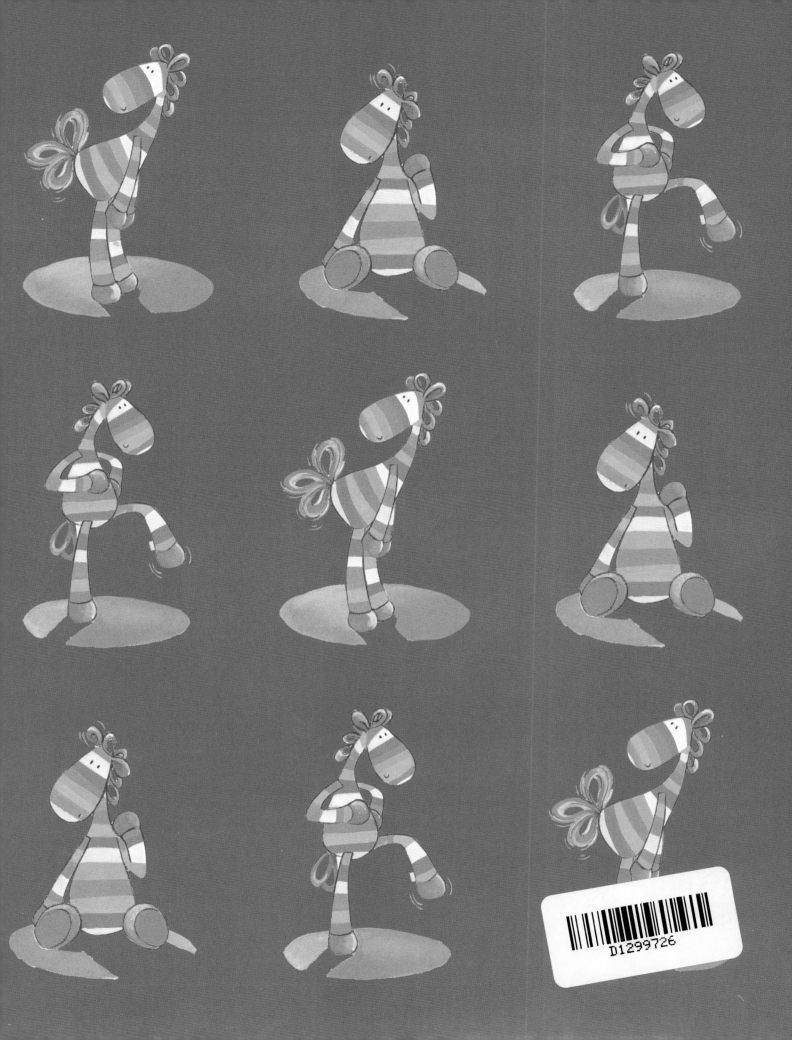

9/5/11

Dear Madi—
Happy belated birthday.
We hope you enjoy
finding your stripes.
Jess, Alex + Ian Pichs.

For Ben

© 2007 by Egmont UK Limited

This 2009 edition published by
Sandy Creek
122 Fifth Avenue
New York, NY 10011

Text copyright © Jim Helmore 2007
Illustrations copyright © Karen Wall 2007

ISBN - 978 1 4351 1590 3

Printed in Singapore
10 9 8 7 6 5 4 3 2 1

WHO ARE YOU, STRIPY HORSE?

Jim Helmore and Karen Wall

ONE STARRY NIGHT,

in a long forgotten shop,

something magical was about to happen . . .

In the tick-tock quiet, a shaft of moonlight tickled the nose of something sleeping. It was a stuffed and stripy horse.

"ACHOO!"

The stripy horse let out an enormous, dusty sneeze and woke himself up.

He shook an ear,

then a leg,

then his tail.

They all seemed to work.

"Hello!" called a hummingbird from the lampshade above. "I've been wondering if you'd ever wake up. My name's Muriel, who are you?"

The stripy horse thought hard but his mind was full of stuffing.

"Well, what do you do?" Muriel persisted.

"Er . . . I can't remember," said the stripy horse looking sad.

"Cheer up," chirped Muriel. "If you
don't know, we could try asking
Ming the Wise. But we'll have to
be careful; he hates being disturbed."

"I wouldn't upset him!"
replied the stripy horse.
"I'm very good with delicate objects!"

"Come on then," twittered Muriel.
"But we'll have to be quick.
The shop opens in a few hours . . ."

"Oops!" cried the stripy horse as he tripped over something squashy.

"Sorry!" said a low, sleepy voice.

"Stripy horse, meet Hermann," chirped Muriel.
"He's a draft catcher."

"Shouldn't you be right next to the door
to stop drafts?" asked
the stripy horse.
"Brrr!" shivered Hermann.
"That sounds chilly!"

"We're off to visit Ming," interrupted Muriel.
"Why don't you come with us?"
asked the stripy horse.
"I'd love to!" said Hermann.

"Look, it's Roly and Pitch!" said Muriel.

"They're salt and pepper pot penguins."

"Ahoy there!" called the penguins.

"And who are you, stripy horse?"

The stripy horse sighed.

"I can't remember."

Roly and Pitch studied the stripy horse carefully in case they could help. "We're seasoned travellers," said the penguins.

"We've seen a lot of things in our time . . .

but nothing quite like you."

Outside, day was beginning to break.

"Come on!" flapped Muriel.

"Time is running out!"

At the front of the shop stood a tall counter.

"Ming lives up there," announced Muriel.
"On Table Top Mountain."

They all looked up.

"How are we supposed to reach him?"
asked the stripy horse.

"Leave it to me!" said Hermann,
and he puffed
and pushed his way up, up, up.

The stripy horse slowly
climbed up Hermann's body.

"I can't look!" cried Roly,
who suddenly felt
very fragile.

When at last they reached the top, the penguins let out a cheer.
"There he is!" cried Pitch.

Fast asleep on his vase, at the top of a very grand stand, sat Ming the Wise.
Carved into the wood below him were two Chinese dragons.

"We're almost out of time! Be careful stripy horse,"
warned Muriel.
"Ming has a terrible temper."

The stripy horse tiptoed forwards.

Suddenly there was a rumbling sound . . .

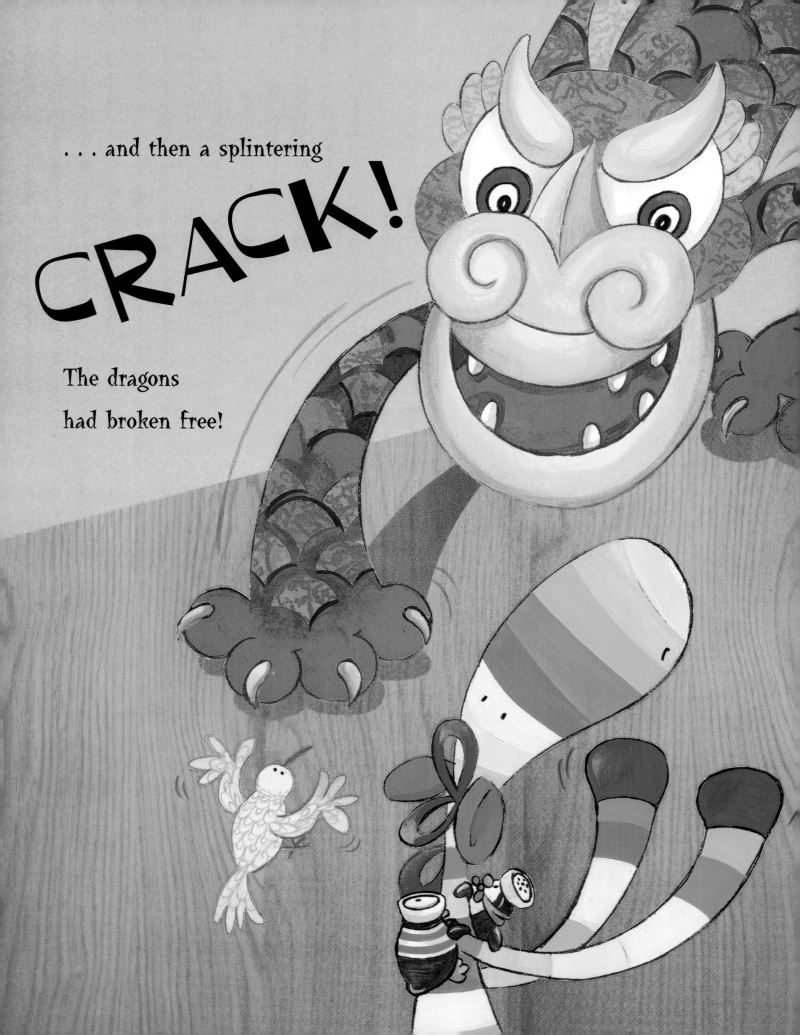

. . . and then a splintering

CRACK!

The dragons
had broken free!

"Keep Back!" they roared.
"No one disturbs the Wise One!"

"What on earth-h-h is going on?" came a hissing voice. Ming frowned down at everyone. "I'm **trying** to s-s-sleep!"

His expression soon changed to horror because . . .

Hermann had puffed  and panted . . .

. . . and pulled himself up onto the counter . . .

. . . and now he was running towards them at slippery speed!

"Don't start without me!" he called.

"Oh no!"

Hermann **crashed** into his friends . . . . who **bumped** into the dragons . . . .

who knocked Ming clean off his stand!

Ming's vase spun in the air.

"Don't worry," cried the stripy horse.

He moved a little to the left,

then a little to the right.

"I'm very good with delicate objects!"

The stripy horse
caught Ming
just in time.

"Thank goodness!"
sighed Muriel.

"I've never been
s-s-so disturbed
in all my life!"
screeched Ming.

"Please, your Wiseness,"
said the stripy horse,
"I only want to ask if you know who I am?"

"Muriel is part of a lampshade,

Hermann is a draft catcher

and Roly and Pitch are salt and pepper pots.

"What am I?
Do I have a name?"

Ming closed his eyes.
"I'm very tired," he yawned,
"so I'll only say this once.

**ALWAYS READ
THE LABEL.**"

And with that,
he went back to sleep.

"Always read the label? What does that mean?
Now I'll never find out who I am."
A single tear trickled from the stripy horse's eye.

"You can have my name if you like," volunteered Hermann.

"Wait a minute!" exclaimed Roly.
"Take a look at this!" shouted Pitch.

They flicked a small label that was sewn into the stripy horse's leg. The label was ratty and old but the penguins could just read what was printed on it . . .

STRIPY HORSE TOY
HAND WASH

"Handwash!" The stripy horse smiled.
"My name is Handwash – and I'm a toy! At last I know who I am!"
"Hurray!" everyone cheered.

As the sun rose in the sky, the stripy horse
and his friends hurried back to their places.
The shop was about to open.

"Thanks for all your help!" he called.

"It was nothing, Handwash," said Muriel.
"That's what friends are for."

The stripy horse looked out of the window.

It was going to be a beautiful day.

FOR

EVAN, TEGAN

AND POPPY

© 2008 by Egmont UK Limited

This 2009 edition published by
Sandy Creek
122 Fifth Avenue
New York, NY 10011

Text copyright © Tim Helmore 2008
Illustrations copyright © Karen Wall 2008

ISBN – 978 1 4351 1590 3
Printed in Singapore
10 9 8 7 6 5 4 3 2 1

KEP LOCKED

5000 pieces

MONKEY P

zle

5000 pieces

150 PIECES

LOOK OUT, STRIPY HORSE!

Jim Helmore and Karen Wall

Magic was at work in the stripy horse's shop.
Magic . . . and mischief!

Nothing
looked
quite
the way
it should.

"**Help!**" barked Hermann, the draft catcher. "I've been tied in a knot!"

"**Goodness!**" twittered Muriel from her lampshade. "I've been scribbled on!"

"**ACHOO!**" sneezed Roly, the saltpot penguin. "I've been filled with pepper."

"And I've been filled with salt," groaned his pepperpot partner, Pitch.

"Oh dear, oh dear!"
Mortice, the lion-shaped lock,
 looked out from his wooden trunk.
 "Someone forgot to lock me up
 and now the monkeys have escaped!"

"Monkeys?" asked
 the stripy horse.

DANGER!
JIGSAW PUZZLES

KEEP LOCKED

"Those **mischievous** monkeys from the monkey puzzle!" growled the lion. "And they've taken my key! What **shall** I do without it?"

"Try this . . ." said Hermann popping a pencil into Mortice's mouth.

DANGER!
JIGSAW PUZZLES

"Mmmmm," chomped the lion.

"Look out, stripy horse!" flapped Muriel.

A monkey darted from the shadows and ran straight towards them.

WHEEEE

"Not so fast, you pesky primate!"
cried Roly and Pitch.

eeee!

"There goes my key!"
roared Mortice.

But the monkey
slipped out
of their net.

"Stop thief!" bellowed Hermann,
as the mischievous monkey swung up and away.

"Oh, they're slippery, those monkeys," sighed the lion.

"Don't worry," said the stripy horse. "I'm very good with slippery objects!"

And he galloped after Hermann.

CRASH!

They were all so busy watching the monkey that they forgot to watch one another!

PLONK!

THUD!

WallOP!

"Well, you won't catch a monkey like that," said Mortice.

"How **are** we supposed to catch them?" asked the stripy horse.

"We must get all the monkeys to stand on top of the jigsaw," explained Mortice. "Then shout, 'ELZZUP YEKNOM' as loudly as we can and the monkeys will be pulled back into the puzzle."

"ELZZUP YEKNOM?" said Hermann. "That sounds like fun!"

"But we'll need to make the jigsaw first," said Pitch. "Come on, Roly!"

"I've had an idea,"
trilled Muriel as
the final pieces
slotted together.
"Follow me everyone . . ."

They all squeezed under the sideboard.

"To get the monkeys back on top of their puzzle," whispered Muriel,

"we'll need something they can't resist."

"What do you mean?" asked Pitch.

"BANANAS!" woofed Hermann.

"Exactly!" said Muriel. "We'll give the monkeys
the biggest banana they've ever seen."
"And where do we get one of those?" asked the stripy horse.
Muriel smiled. "Wait and see!"

"What do you think, everyone?" chuckled Hermann.

"Are you **sure** this is going to work?" grumbled Mortice.

The friends crawled back under the sideboard and waited. All was silent except for the ticking of the cuckoo clock.

Then a shadow darted across the room.

Slowly, slowly one of the monkeys stole into view . . . then another,

Everyone held
their breath.

and another   until soon six monkeys were   creeping towards . . .

"EL..."
began Roly.

"Wait!" hushed Muriel.
"Don't shout
until they're **all**
on top of the puzzle."

The monkeys crept closer.

"**Now!**" whispered the stripy horse.

"ELZZUP YEKNOM!"

everyone cried.

FLASH!

BANG!

WHIZZ!

The shop lit up
with sparkling,
crackling light.

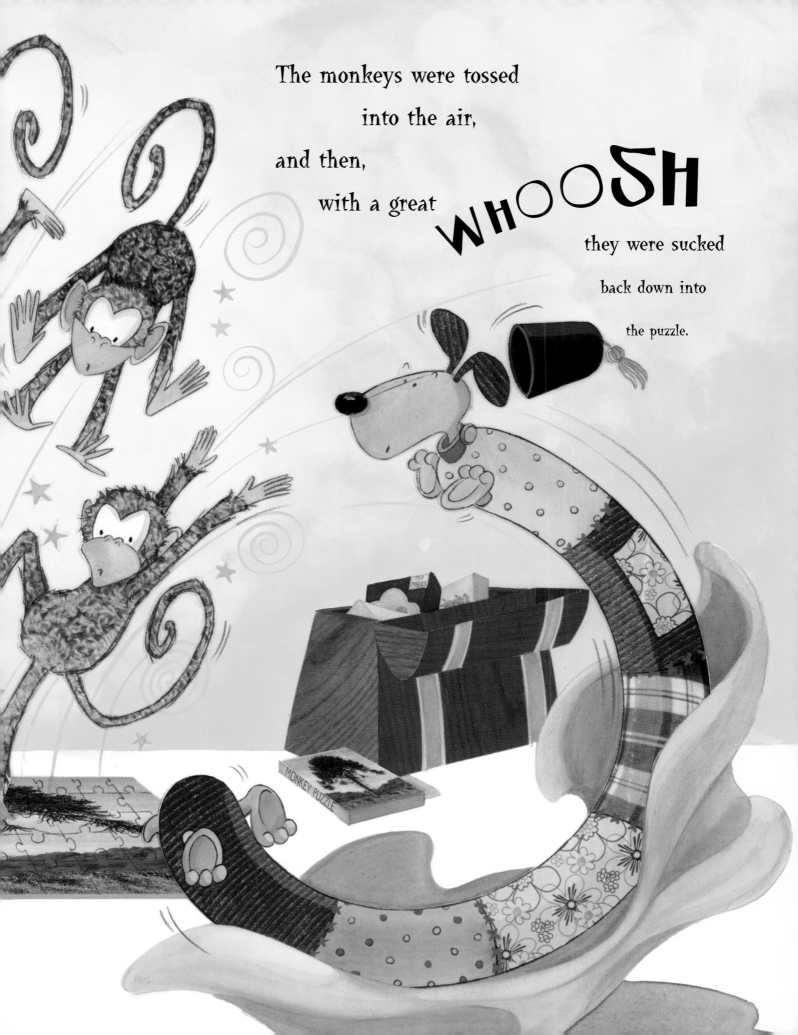

The monkeys were tossed
into the air,
and then,
with a great WHOOSH
they were sucked
back down into
the puzzle.

"Quickly!" said Muriel.
"Put the puzzle back
inside the trunk before
those monkeys get up
to any more tricks."

"But we can't lock
the puzzle away
until I get my key back,"
said Mortice.
"**Where** can it be?"

"CUCKOO!"

It was
five o'clock.
The cuckoo at the top of the clock
shot in and out, five noisy times.

"There it is!"
flapped Muriel.

The lion's missing key
dropped from
the cuckoo's beak.

"Look **out below!**"

called Muriel.

"**Got you!**"

said the stripy horse as he caught the shiny key.

Click!
The stripy horse turned the key
in the lion's mouth
and the monkey puzzle
was safely locked away.

DANGER! JIGSAW PUZZLES

KEEP LOCKED

"Mmmmm," chomped Mortice.
"Thank you, stripy horse. Pencils
are all well and good, but you
can't beat a nice tasty key."

Day was breaking as the
friends settled back
into their places
for a well-earned rest.

And all was quiet in the shop once more . . .

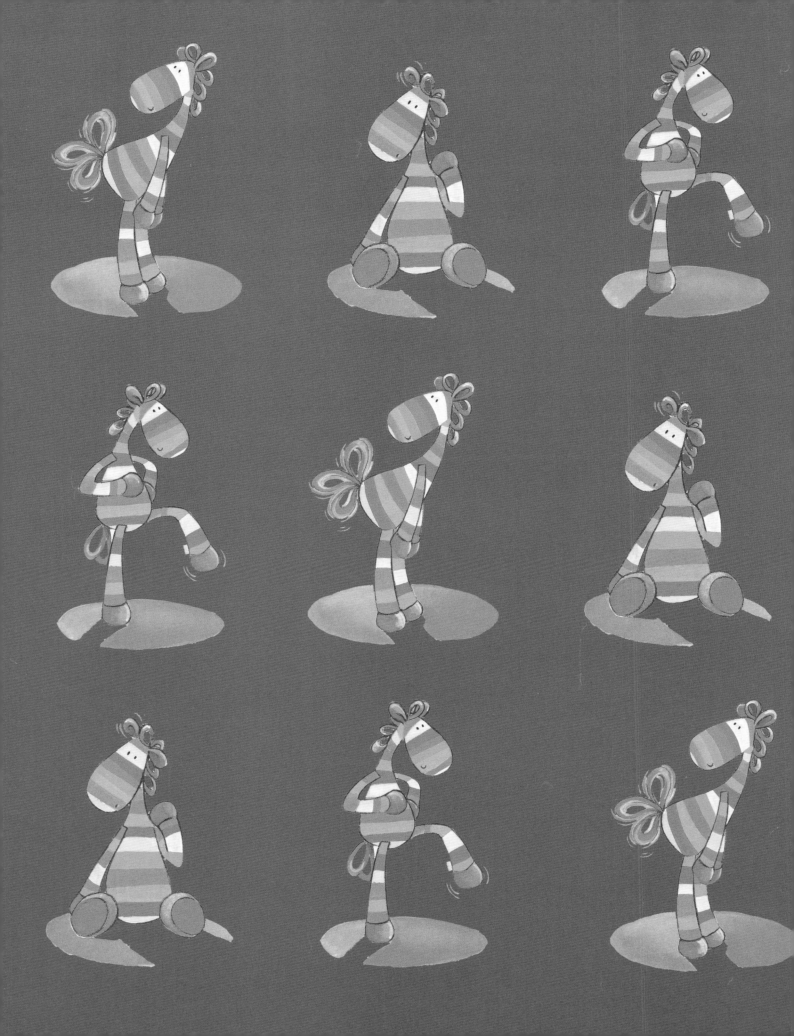